x971.5 Campb.K

Campbell, Kumari.

Destination Saint John /

DATE DUE	
JUN 4 - 2003	
JAN 3 0 2007 2-26-07	

DEMCO, INC. 38-2931

DESTINATION SAINT JOHN

CANADA
UNITED STATES
MEXICO
Quebec
Quebec
Gulf of St. Lawrence
N
W
E
S
CANADA
St. John River
New Brunswick
Prince Edward Island
Maine
Fredericton
Kennebecasis River
Northumberland Strait
St. Croix River
Saint John
UNITED STATES
Bay of Fundy
Nova Scotia
Halifax
Digby
Legend
Port City
0
50
100 miles
0
50
100 kilometers
ATLANTIC OCEAN

DESTINATION
SAINT JOHN

by Kumari Campbell

Lerner Publications Company

PHOTO ACKNOWLEDGMENTS

Cover photograph by © Rob Roy Reproductions. All inside photos courtesy of © Rob Roy Reproductions, pp. 5, 8, 12, 14, 17, 19 (bottom), 21, 22, 24, 46, 59, 66, 68 (both), 70, 73; Saint John Port Corporation, pp. 6, 9, 10, 13, 15, 16–17, 18, 19 (top), 20, 22–23, 51, 52, 53 (both), 55 (top), 56, 57, 75; © Buddy Mays/Travel Stock, pp. 6, 45, 60, 62, 67, 71, 76; Artwork by Lewis Parker, collection University of Cape Breton, photograph by Michael Reppa, p. 28; Claude Picard, Artist/Commissioned by Canadian Heritage (Parks Canada), Atlantic Region, p. 31; Corbis-Bettmann, p. 33; Confederation Life Gallery of Canadian History, p. 34; D. Lynch, Heritage Saint John collection, PIRP #6814, p. 36; National Archives of Canada/Negative #C–116960, p. 37; Heritage Saint John collection, PIRP #3716, p. 40; The Provincial Archives of New Brunswick, p. 41; I. Brown, Heritage Saint John collection, PIRP #6678, p. 42; Heritage Saint John collection, PIRP #465, p. 43; Reuters/Mike Theiler/Archive Photos, p. 50; Irving Oil Company, p. 55; Tourism New Brunswick, p. 63; © Voscar, The Maine Photographer, pp. 64, 69, 74; © James P. Rowan, p. 72. Maps by Ortelius Design.

Copyright © 1998 by Lerner Publications Company,
Minneapolis, Minnesota, U.S.A.

All rights reserved. International copyright secured. No part of this book may be reproduced, stored in a retrieval system, or transmitted in any form or by any means—electronic, mechanical, photocopying, recording, or otherwise—without the prior written permission of Lerner Publications Company, except for the inclusion of brief quotations in an acknowledged review.

Website address: www.lernerbooks.com

LIBRARY OF CONGRESS CATALOGING-IN-PUBLICATION DATA

Campbell, Kumari.
    Destination Saint John / by Kumari Campbell.
      p. cm. — (Port cities of North America)
    Includes index.
    Summary: Discusses the geography, history, economy, and daily life of the eastern Canadian port of Saint John.
    ISBN 0-8225-2785-5 (lib. bdg. : alk. paper)
    1. Saint John (N.B.)—Juvenile literature. [1. Saint John (N.B.)] I. Title. II. Series.
F1044.5.S14C26   1998
971.5'32—dc21   96-48741

Manufactured in the United States of America
1 2 3 4 5 6 – JR – 03 02 01 00 99 98

The glossary that begins on page 76 gives definitions of words shown in **bold type** in the text.

CONTENTS

CHAPTER ONE	Lay of the Land	7
CHAPTER TWO	Saint John's History	27
CHAPTER THREE	The Port at Work	47
CHAPTER FOUR	Loyalist City	61

Glossary	76
Pronunciation Guide	77
Index	78
About the Author	80

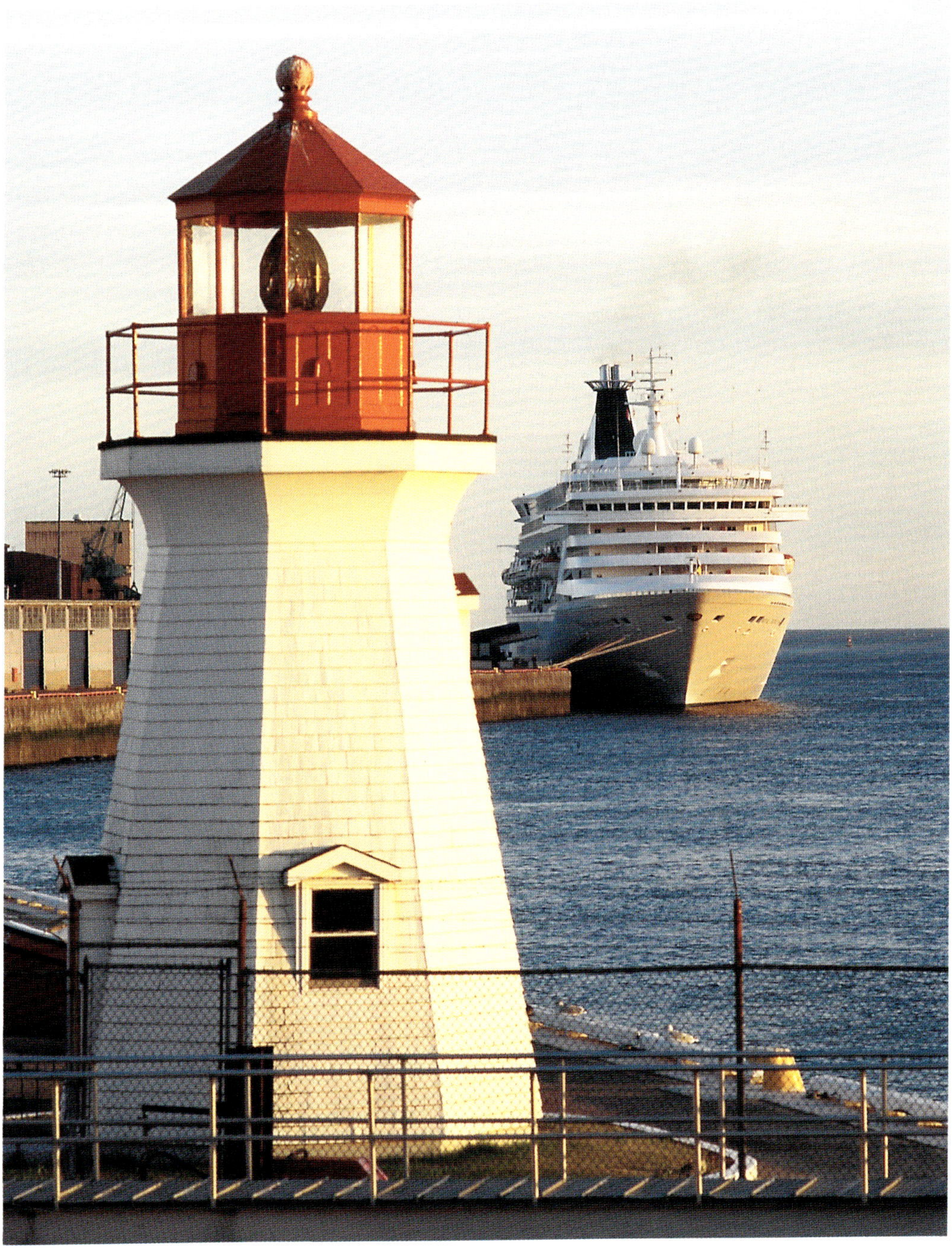

CHAPTER ONE

LAY OF THE LAND

Description of the Port ▶ Ranking among Canada's top ports, Saint John, New Brunswick, has long been one of the most important ports on North America's eastern seaboard (Atlantic coast). The port is at the mouth of the St. John River on the southern coast of New Brunswick, one of Canada's three Maritime Provinces. These provinces, which also include Nova Scotia and Prince Edward Island, border the Atlantic Ocean. Nova Scotia lies to the southeast of New Brunswick across the Bay of Fundy. To the east of New Brunswick, across the Northumberland Strait (a narrow passageway in the Gulf of St. Lawrence), is Prince Edward Island. On New Brunswick's northern boundary is the province of Quebec and to the west lies the U.S. state of Maine.

A cruise ship calls at Saint John, New Brunswick (facing page), *which ranks among Canada's top five ports.*

The office buildings in downtown Saint John look out over the port.

On the southern shores of New Brunswick, rugged hills slope down to tidal marshes, where the waters of the Bay of Fundy moderate the province's coastal climate. Winter temperatures along the coast tend to be several degrees warmer and summer temperatures to be cooler than they are in the interior of New Brunswick. Most of the precipitation in coastal communities comes as rain and fog rather than in the form of snow and ice. In addition, the high salt content and constant tidal action of bay waters prevent ice formation in the winter. As an ice-free port, Saint John is open for business throughout the winter months and operates year-round.

Offering year-round service is one factor behind the port's success and growth over the years. So is the fact that Saint John lies closer to major North American markets than any other eastern Canadian port. With short overland distances to markets in the New England states and in the provinces of central Canada,

> The ferry trip across the Bay of Fundy from Saint John to Digby, Nova Scotia, takes 2.5 hours, while the overland route takes 7 hours.

Saint John is a shipping and receiving point for cargoes to and from these areas. And the port's location on the Bay of Fundy, which shelters Saint John's harbor from the open waters of the Atlantic Ocean, offers safe docking for vessels.

Port authorities also credit Saint John's diverse facilities and services for its success. For example, the port handles many different types of cargo, including various **bulk cargoes,** containerized shipments, and roll-on/roll-off (ro-ro) traffic. Saint John also hosts a busy schedule of cruise-ship visits, provides a daily car-ferry service across the Bay of Fundy, and supports a commercial fishery as well as recreational fishing and pleasure-craft activities. Moreover, the port is the home of one of North America's largest shipyards.

Ro-ro vessels provide an easy way to load and unload cargo. Trucks cross specially designed ramps directly onto ships to drop off or pick up their loads.

Saint John Harbor covers a total area of 269 acres. It houses 27 berths, or docking spaces, with a total of 15,748 feet of docking frontage. The harbor also includes more than 1 million square feet of storage space and 116 acres of open area that can be used for various purposes. The harbor has three main sections—the Main Harbor, Courtenay Bay, and the Outer Harbor. The wide Outer Harbor narrows into a U shape as it wraps around the city's main **peninsula,** which juts out into the water. The western arm of the U forms the Main Harbor, while the eastern arm forms Courtenay Bay.

An aerial view reveals the Main Harbor and Courtenay Bay, which form the hub of the Port of Saint John.

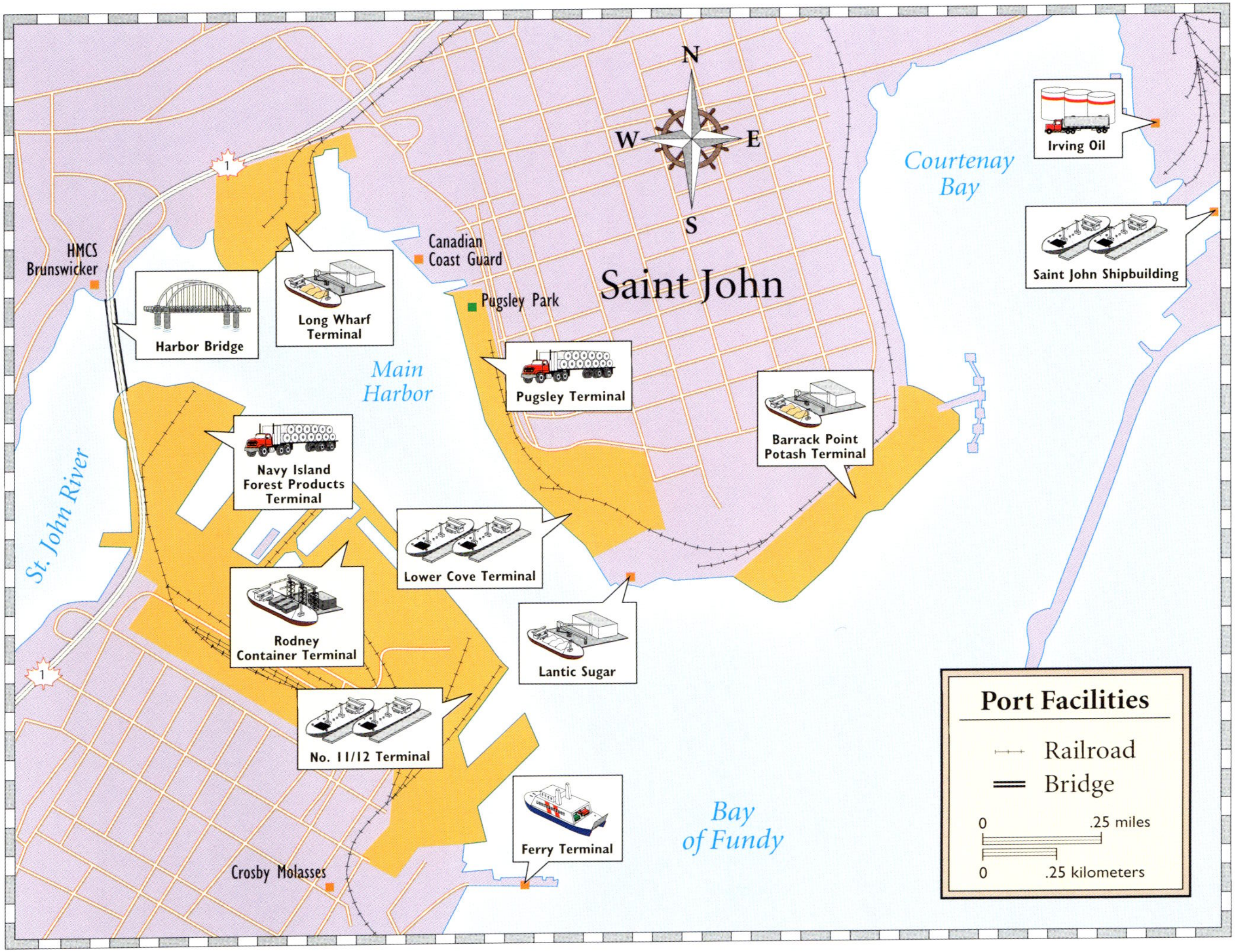
Port Facilities
Railroad
Bridge
0 .25 miles
0 .25 kilometers
N
S
W
E
Saint John
Courtenay Bay
Bay of Fundy
Main Harbor
St. John River
Irving Oil
Saint John Shipbuilding
Barrack Point Potash Terminal
Pugsley Terminal
Pugsley Park
Canadian Coast Guard
Long Wharf Terminal
Harbor Bridge
HMCS Brunswicker
Navy Island Forest Products Terminal
Lower Cove Terminal
Lantic Sugar
Rodney Container Terminal
No. 11/12 Terminal
Ferry Terminal
Crosby Molasses
1
1

Navigating Tidal Waters

Saint John's tidal waters are among the port's most unique features. Because the tides rise and fall four times a day, the water level in the harbor goes through sharp changes every few hours. To complicate matters even more, the St. John River constantly empties large amounts of water into the harbor. During the two high tides each day, the depth of the harbor can rise between 22 feet and 28 feet above the low-water level. During each day's two low tides, the harbor depth may stay at the low-water level or rise as high as 7 feet above it.

The depth of the port's main channel is 28 feet at low-water level, although the water at the harbor's berths is deeper so that ships can anchor safely even during low tide. Ships that are unable to navigate the channel at low tide simply wait until high tide to do so.

You would think that such sharp and frequent variations in water depth would make it very difficult for harbor pilots to steer ships in and out of the harbor. But with good directions

Saint John is a tidal port, where water levels can change dramatically throughout the day. Most ships take advantage of the deeper water levels during high tide to maneuver in and out of the harbor. This ship (below) *rests at a dock on Courtenay Bay during low tide.*

Much of Saint John's navigational equipment is computerized. The flow of water traffic is monitored from the time ships enter the Bay of Fundy until they leave.

> ➤ The Bay of Fundy has some of the world's highest tides. At high tide, the water level may rise as much as 56 feet higher than the water level at low tide.

A Tour of the Main Harbor

from the harbormaster, the pilots manage to dock ships easily. The tidal window—a period of time on either side of high tide—lasts about five hours, so ships use this time to move in and out of their berths. The harbormaster watches the level of the tides very closely and keeps careful track of the number of ships moving in and out of the harbor each day. This port official knows how long it takes to move a ship in or out of every berth and what water depth each ship requires. With input from ship pilots, the harbormaster decides which vessels will be moved each day and what time of day they will make the trip. Ships are allowed to anchor in a special area of the Outer Harbor while they await their turn to dock.

➤ As a multiuse harbor, the Port of Saint John accommodates ships and cargoes that require a wide range of handling methods. The seven terminals owned by the Saint John Port Corporation, which operates the port, each have

Lantic Sugar, Canada's largest sugar refinery, processes and packages imported sugar.

different handling capabilities, storage capacities, and docking facilities so that they can cater to as many needs as possible.

Six of the port-owned terminals lie within the Main Harbor. Lower Cove Terminal, located on the eastern side of the harbor, functions as an all-purpose terminal for various types of cargoes, including petroleum and sugar. At the outer end of the terminal is the privately owned Lantic Sugar refinery. Lantic Sugar imports raw, brown sugar from Australia and Cuba and refines and packages the sugar for delivery to eastern Canadian markets. Workers usually need four to five days to unload a shipment of raw sugar, which ranges from 27,500 to 38,500 tons. Each year Saint John imports about 275,000 tons of raw sugar.

A pipeline links Lower Cove Terminal to a nearby petroleum tank farm (a collection of several gigantic holding tanks) for storing gasoline and other imported petroleum fuels. Trucks carry the fuels from the tank farm to vendors throughout New Brunswick. Lower Cove Terminal also provides a docking area for cruise ships sailing from the United States and Europe. Every year between 8 and 15 ships stop at the port, bringing close to 20,000 visitors to Saint John. The passengers spend their time in

> ➤ Lower Cove Terminal really was a cove (inlet) at one time. Workers filled it in to make 18 acres of land for wharves and terminal buildings.

port shopping, eating at local restaurants, or touring the city's famous parks and historical sites.

Next to Lower Cove Terminal is Pugsley Terminal. Like its neighbor, this all-purpose terminal can accommodate many types of cargoes.

Workers load paper rolls onto a ship at Pugsley Terminal.

One of its main uses is for shipping forest products—a major New Brunswick export. As one of the older terminals at the port, Pugsley Terminal has narrower **aprons** than the newer terminals. In the early days of shipping, longshoremen (dockworkers) moved all cargo manually, so the distances between ships and dockside storage areas were short. Nowadays cranes and other heavy machinery, which need more room to move around, handle much of the cargo.

Long Wharf, the last terminal on the east side of the Main Harbor, is also the oldest section of the port. The original wooden wharf has been replaced by a stronger, fire-resistant concrete structure. Ships docking at this terminal carry salt from New Brunswick to states in New England, where road crews spread the salt to break up ice in the winter. Long Wharf Terminal has a rail track that comes right to the apron of the dock, allowing bulk cargo to be loaded directly from railcars onto vessels. This convenient method of loading means that the cargo doesn't have to be unloaded and stored in a warehouse while it is waiting for a ship to arrive.

On the western side of the Main Harbor, across from Long Wharf Terminal, lies the busy Navy Island Forest Products Terminal. Seven deepwater berths provide ample docking space from which forestry products, such as baled pulp, newsprint, fiberboard, and lumber, are exported. Although a large portion of these products is produced right in New Brunswick, many are freighted in by railcars from as far away as the western Canadian province of Manitoba, as well as from New England. The Port of Saint John handles the largest volume of forestry products—more than 1 million tons—on the Atlantic seaboard. And because forestry products require a lot of handling en route to market, they provide a large number of jobs for residents in the Saint John area.

The Navy Island terminal is the cleanest and one of the most high-tech areas of the port. Computers keep track of the large quantities of wood products that move in and out of the terminal warehouses. Massive storage sheds with

▶ The HMCS Brunswicker is located beside Long Wharf Terminal. The Brunswicker building is the site of the Canadian naval reserve, where members train to operate patrol vessels.

concrete floors supply 525,000 square feet of storage space for neatly baled wood pulp and newsprint. Clean, dry storage is very important for these products because they can be easily damaged by moisture. In addition, mud or grease from large trucks can ruin newsprint. Therefore, a protective coating covers the floors, which special street-sweeping machines clean constantly.

Most forest products at the terminal are loaded onto vessels by the roll-on/roll-off method, whereby trucks hauling loaded trailers called maffies drive onto ramps that lead directly into the holds of the vessels. The ro-ro method is much easier and faster than using cranes to move cargo from the dock onto ships. After the trucks are inside the ship, large forklifts called liftjacks unload the cargo from the maffies.

The same tidal action that faces ships moving in and out of Saint John Harbor can cause problems for a vessel's ro-ro ramps. These ramps, which are usually only about 10 feet long, rest on the ship just a few inches above water level. When the tide is low, the ramps sit lower than at high tide and become too steep for trucks to drive on. So port staff have designed a special

At Long Wharf Terminal, elongated conveyor belts load salt onto a ship (above) *at the rate of 1,320 tons per hour. A barge stacked high with logs* (below) *heads for the Navy Island Forest Products Terminal. The terminal services New Brunswick's many pulp and paper mills.*

Trucks delivering cargo to the Port of Saint John rely on floating docks (left) *to drive onto ro-ro vessels at low tide. Containers* (facing page top) *are convenient because they hold large quantities of cargo and are easily moved from ship to truck or train. Specialized cranes called* **gantry cranes** *(facing page bottom) transfer containers to and from ships.*

200-foot-long floating ramp, with one end permanently connected to the dock and the other end linked to a barge. When a ship is loaded at low tide, the ship's ramp is simply connected to the barge. Because the barge always floats at the same level as the ship, the ship's ramp stays flat. Loaded trucks at the port can then safely drive along the gently sloping floating ramp to the barge, across the barge and onto the ship's ramp, and from there into the ship's hold.

In addition to ro-ro ships, many side-loader vessels visit the Navy Island terminal each year. These ships have complex elevator systems built right into the side of the ship. The elevators enable crews to load and unload cargo directly between the wharf apron and the vessels without using ramps. During a typical loading operation, the elevator is raised from the ship's hold to dock level, where cargo is transferred onto the vessel. The elevator is then lowered into the hold, and the cargo is unloaded.

Next to the Navy Island facility is the Rodney Container Terminal, another highly specialized

> ➤ The shipping industry measures container traffic in 20-foot equivalent units (TEUs). One TEU represents a container that is 20 feet long, 8 feet wide, and 8.5 feet or 9.5 feet high.

terminal. Containers are large, rectangular metal boxes used for shipping all kinds of cargoes around the world. Workers pack everything from french fries to electrical equipment into these containers. Because containers are all the same size, they are very easy to stack inside ships and on docks. They also provide a safe method of transport because they are strong and protect cargo from damage and vandalism. For these reasons, container shipping has become an increasingly popular way of moving goods.

The Rodney Container Terminal occupies an area of about 45 acres and handles up to 200,000 containers each year. Flatbed railcars bring containers from all across Canada to Saint John, where workers transfer the containers onto ships with the help of cranes. Vessels deliver containers to a variety of markets around the world. Special refrigerated containers called reefers arrive at the port filled with french fries from Prince Edward Island or dairy products from Quebec. These commodities are exported to Caribbean markets such as Puerto Rico and Trinidad. The reefers return to Saint John with cargoes such as alcoholic and nonalcoholic beverages.

The terminal is equipped with gantry cranes (enormous cranes the size of multistoried buildings) for moving containers on and off ships. The cranes travel back and forth along the terminal apron on wide tracks resembling railway tracks. Crane operators lift containers directly onto ships from flatbed railcars that move along a rail track extending onto the apron. The terminal also has space to store large numbers of containers in dockside racks that can hold several layers of containers. Reefer containers are plugged into electrical outlets while they sit at the terminal. Just like at the forestry products terminal, computers keep track of all storage information at the Rodney Container Terminal.

The last of the terminals owned by the Saint John Port Corporation is known simply as the No. 11/12 Terminal, because it houses berths 11 and 12. This all-purpose terminal handles **general cargo** and bulk cargo. Like the Rodney and the Long Wharf terminals, Berth No. 12 has a rail track on its apron so that cargo can be moved directly between trains and ships. Some of the cargo that passes through this terminal is liquid bulk, such as molasses from the Caribbean island of Barbados. Unloaded into storage tanks owned by Crosby Molasses Company, the molasses is refined at Crosby's refinery in Saint John and is then packaged and sold across Canada. The terminal also handles imported fish meal from Iceland and Peru. Fish farmers in New Brunswick's aquaculture industry buy the meal to feed the salmon and other fish they raise for commercial distribution.

Workers at the Port of Saint John unload liquid bulk products by pumping them through large pipes into storage tanks. Each type of liquid bulk has its own set of handling requirements. For instance, gasoline is monitored very closely during unloading to protect against leaks that could lead to fires, explosions, or environmental contamination. Molasses, on the other hand, has to be kept warm to flow through the pipes.

A supertanker transfers petroleum to an offshore monobuoy (floating dock) at the Canaport Marine Terminal.

On the west side of the Main Harbor, beyond the No. 11/12 facilities, lies the ferry terminal that offers daily automobile ferry service across the Bay of Fundy. An important transportation link between New Brunswick and Nova Scotia, the ferry trip is 362 miles shorter than the overland route between the two provinces. Each year the ferry service transports more than 200,000 passengers and more than 80,000 vehicles, about one-third of which are transport trucks.

A Tour of Courtenay Bay and the Outer Harbor

Barrack Point Potash Terminal is the only port-owned facility on Courtenay Bay. This terminal is dedicated solely to storing and shipping potash, a mineral used to make fertilizer. The potash, which workers unearth in nearby New Brunswick mines, is a red-brown grainy substance much like sand. A bulk cargo, potash

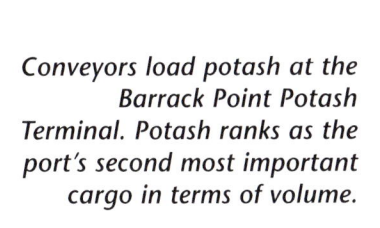

> Barrack Point gets its name from the fact that this section of the port was occupied by military barracks in the early 1800s.

Conveyors load potash at the Barrack Point Potash Terminal. Potash ranks as the port's second most important cargo in terms of volume.

21

arrives at the terminal in railcars, each with a capacity of about 110 tons. Warehouses store the potash until bulk carriers arrive for loading. Conveyor belts transfer the potash into the holds of the carriers at a rate of about 3,000 tons per hour. The potash then continues on its journey to Mexico, South America, Europe, and other global markets.

The remaining facilities in the Courtenay Bay section of the harbor are private operations. The most important of these are Irving Oil, Irving Paper, and Saint John Shipbuilding, all owned by the Irving family—one of New Brunswick's leading families of industrialists. The Saint John Shipbuilding company is one of the largest in Canada. The facility offers five **dry docks** for ship repair and has equipment for building a wide range of ships, including naval frigates and commercial fleets.

The Outer Harbor lies outside the port's two **breakwaters.** The shorter of the two barriers is the Partridge Island breakwater (3,281 feet), which extends into the Bay of Fundy from the west side of the harbor to Partridge Island. The longer Courtenay Bay breakwater (5,249 feet) lies closer to the Main Harbor and shelters

The Irving Oil refinery in East Saint John processes imported and domestic crude oil into gasoline and a variety of other petroleum products.

22

A crowd gathers at a dry dock to witness the launching of a new ship.

Courtenay Bay from the waters of the Outer Harbor. A light at the end of the breakwater along with channel buoys in the water mark the way to the Courtenay Bay channel.

Because harbors are naturally much shallower than the ocean, crews dredge (dig) navigational channels between the ocean and the docking berths to provide ships with the water depth they need for navigation. Ships use these channels, much as cars use roads, to travel in and out of harbors. Saint John Harbor has two channels, one leading to the Main Harbor and the other to Courtenay Bay.

The Outer Harbor provides temporary anchorage space for ships awaiting berths, emergency anchorage for ships with problems such as fuel leaks or other damage, and emergency beaching areas for ships that have to be abandoned because of fire and other emergencies. The Canaport Marine Terminal, a monobuoy (floating dock) owned by Irving Oil, is located in this area. All the crude (unrefined) oil imported into Saint John is unloaded at this terminal and piped to the Irving Oil refinery in East Saint John. The Outer Harbor is also a commercial fishing ground and a safe boating area for sailboats, speedboats, and other pleasure craft.

▶ Workers at Saint John Shipbuilding at the Port of Saint John construct oil rigs, icebreakers, commercial cargo vessels, and state-of-the-art naval frigates.

23

DREDGING

Ever since inventors created steel-hulled ships in the late 1800s, dredging has been necessary at many ports to provide the deepwater channels that big, heavy ships need for navigating. In a tidal harbor such as Saint John, dredging is even more important because the tides bring large amounts of sand into the water each day. The St. John River also deposits a lot of silt into harbor waters. And in the spring, melting snow and ice flow into the waterway, causing a **freshet** (a rise or overflowing of a river). The freshet brings with it even more silt than the river normally carries.

Federal guidelines strictly regulate harbor dredging. Planning for the annual dredging process begins in January, when biologists test sediment samples from the harbor floor for contaminants. If the tests show levels that are not harmful, the dredged material can be dumped in the ocean, as long as the port has received an ocean-dumping permit from the Canadian government. If the contaminant level is high, however, the material is dumped on land in diked (contained) enclosures to protect the surrounding area. Since dumping on land costs seven times more than ocean dumping, the port does all it can to keep the harbor as free of contaminants as possible.

Dredging begins in July, well after the end of the annual spring freshet. Before, during, and after the dredging process, hydrographic surveys keep track of water depth to ensure safe navigation. Each year crews remove about 727,000 cubic yards of material during the dredging process, costing about $2 million Canadian (U.S. $1.5 million).

Protecting the Environment

Dredging is only one activity the port corporation undertakes each year to maintain the harbor for all its users. Another major concern is protecting the natural environment. The port has developed an environmental plan to make sure port users obey all federal, provincial, and municipal environmental regulations. The plan also addresses all possible environmental threats, no matter how small.

Biologists conduct annual environmental audits (checks) around the port. Each operation at the port receives a detailed audit at least once every five years. Through these audits, the port corporation can find out whether or not each operation is obeying the rules. As a result of these strict regulations, the port has never had a serious environmental emergency.

In 1993 the city of Saint John undertook a major study of the harbor's natural environment and designed a plan for treating the city's wastewater, most of which goes into the harbor. Since then, both the port corporation and the city have spent a lot of money on improving the harbor's marine environment, mostly through upgrading the treatment of sewage. The port also has developed a marine contingency plan, with detailed instructions on how to handle all kinds of marine emergencies, from fires to oil and chemical spills.

Each year the Port of Saint John handles thousands of ships and more than 20 million tons of cargo. To protect this valuable part of New Brunswick's economy, port users and the Saint John Port Corporation are committed to working together to maintain a clean, safe, and successful port.

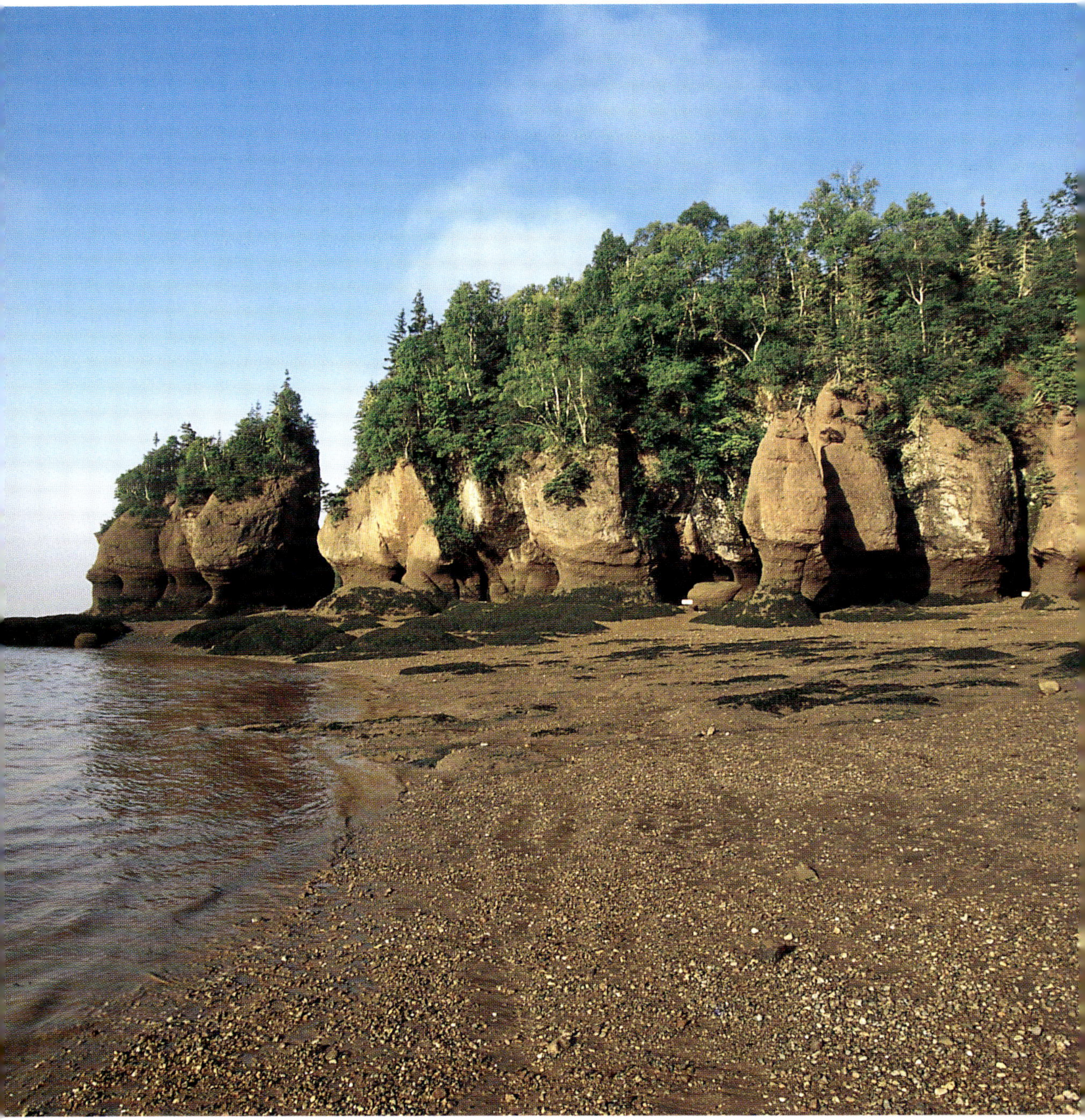

CHAPTER TWO

SAINT JOHN'S HISTORY

Early Inhabitants ▶ Scientists believe that the earliest known human footprints in the Saint John area were left by the Micmac, an Eastern Woodlands Algonquian people who inhabited most of the Canadian Maritime region about 2,000 years ago. Another Eastern Algonquian people, the Maliseet, originally lived in what is now the eastern part of Maine. European exploration and settlement on their lands during the early 1600s, however, pushed the Maliseet eastward into present-day New Brunswick. The Maliseet were the first permanent residents of the St. John River valley.

The powerful tidal waters of the Bay of Fundy carved giant stone formations known as the Flowerpot Rocks (facing page) *at Hopewell Cape in southeastern New Brunswick. The bay waters provided fertile fishing grounds for the region's earliest inhabitants.*

The Maliseet lived in wigwams, which are circular or oval-shaped structures made with wooden poles and covered with birch bark or animal hides. During the warm months of the year, women grew crops of corn, beans, and squash in the fertile soil of the river valley. Men fished along the coast during these months and headed inland during the winter to hunt and trap.

The Maliseet and the Micmac were peaceful peoples. Since they had common Eastern Algonquian roots, they shared many similarities in their languages and customs. While the Maliseet were among the earliest Native peoples to settle permanently in one place and to grow crops, the Micmac were nomadic, moving across their territory according to the seasons. During the summer months, the Micmac lived on the coast, fishing and gathering oysters and digging for clams along the seashore. In the

The Micmac were a hunting and gathering people. They relied on the resources of their forested, well-watered surroundings for food and for the materials to build their homes and to make clothing, canoes, and other necessities of daily life.

> ➤ A Maliseet village called Ouangondy was located on a little island in the mouth of the Saint John Harbor. Later known as Navy Island, the landform was eventually connected to the port as part of the Navy Island Forest Products Terminal.
>
> ➤ The Maliseet people called the St. John River Woolastook, which means "goodly river."

fall, the communities moved inland and lived in wigwams in the forests, where they were more protected from harsh winter weather. The women gathered berries, nuts, and seeds that could be stored for the winter. The men hunted moose and caribou to provide a winter supply of meat. Craftspeople used animal hides and bones for making clothes, blankets, bags, boxes, jewelry, buttons, and many other items of daily life.

Because much of the land was heavily wooded and roads did not exist, traveling overland was very difficult. The Micmac and the Maliseet built birchbark canoes to navigate up and down the rivers to other villages and settlements. They often traded with other groups. For instance, a Micmac band might trade animal skins for corn and beans grown by a Maliseet band.

French Explorers and the Founding of Acadia

➤ In 1534 and 1535, French navigator Jacques Cartier led two expeditions across the Atlantic Ocean, hoping to find a western route to China. Instead he discovered the lands surrounding what were later named the Gulf of St. Lawrence and the St. Lawrence River, all of which Cartier claimed for France.

After Cartier's voyages, French crews sailed across the Atlantic each year to fish in the gulf waters, which were teeming with a variety of fish. During the summer, the French fishers camped along the coastal areas of what became Prince Edward Island and Newfoundland. In the fall, they returned to France with their catches, either sun-dried or preserved in barrels of salt water. During the months they spent in

North America, the French fishers met encampments of Micmac who were also fishing along the coast. Soon the French began trading metal dishes, pots, and tools with the Native peoples in exchange for pelts and skins.

In 1603 King Henry IV of France asked Pierre du Gua de Monts to lead an expedition to the French possessions in North America. The king also sent Samuel de Champlain, the royal cartographer (mapmaker). Along with a group of settlers, the expedition set sail in two ships, one of which was filled with goods to trade with any other settlers they might encounter.

Arriving at the mouth of the Woolastook River on the Feast of St. John the Baptist (June 24) in 1604, de Monts named the waterway the St. John River. But instead of settling on the banks of the St. John, the expedition set up its headquarters on a tiny island in the St. Croix River to the west. While the ships returned to France, de Monts and 80 settlers stayed on. The winter was harsh, with ice so thick that the island was cut off from the mainland. By spring 36 members of the party had died of a disease called scurvy. De Monts immediately moved his headquarters across the Bay of Fundy to Port Royal, which became the first permanent French settlement in North America.

The French-speaking settlers named the territory L'Acadie, or Acadia. The territory included present-day Nova Scotia, New Brunswick, Prince Edward Island, and a small part of the state of Maine. The residents of Acadia called themselves Acadians and worked hard to settle their new homeland. They fished in the Bay of Fundy, built **dikes** to hold back water along the coastal lowlands, and grew crops in the fertile tidal marshes.

The Maliseet in the region befriended the Acadians and taught them how to survive in the harsh North American climate. They introduced the newcomers to edible plants and wildlife and showed them which plants and herbs to use for medicinal purposes. The Native people also taught the Acadians how to build birchbark canoes for traveling the rivers and how to fashion snowshoes for walking across deep snow in winter. In return, the Acadians taught the Maliseet their language and their

Acadian farmers grew a variety of crops, including hay, corn, wheat, rye, oats, and flax. They also raised livestock such as cattle, sheep, and pigs.

music and dances. The communities also became trading partners. In exchange for furs from Native hunters, the Acadians offered metal utensils, guns, and other manufactured goods.

In 1621 the British laid claim to Acadia. This led to long-term feuding between the French and the British over control of North American lands. In 1713, after a lengthy war, Britain and France signed the Treaty of Utrecht and agreed to divide up the land between them. But the feuding didn't stop. Both countries wanted control of what is now New Brunswick, so they each built a fort at the boundary between what later became Nova Scotia and New Brunswick. In 1755 the British captured the French fort, and the French retreated to Louisbourg Fortress on Île Royale (Cape Breton Island, part of present-day Nova Scotia).

Although their lands lay in British-held territory, the Acadians viewed themselves as independent of both the British and the French. But the British were convinced that in the event of a dispute between the two nations, the French-descended Acadians would side with France. To prevent this, the British ordered the Acadians to sign an oath of loyalty to Britain. When the Acadians refused, the British forcibly shipped them south to other British colonies in North America.

By the conclusion of the Seven Years' War (1756–1763)—a later stage of the conflict between France and Britain—the British had gained control of all French territory in what is now Canada. After the war, Acadians slowly

British North America

▶ The earliest European settlement at the mouth of the St. John River dates back to a French trading post built by Charles de La Tour in the early 1630s. The post was later fortified and named Fort La Tour. This trading post was the predecessor of the Port of Saint John.

▶ The 1713 Treaty of Utrecht gave mainland Nova Scotia, New Brunswick, and Newfoundland to Britain. France received Quebec, Prince Edward Island, and Cape Breton Island (part of present-day Nova Scotia).

In the mid-1700s, British officers rounded up Acadians, burned their farms, and forcibly deported them to the British colonies in what later became the United States. Many Acadians eventually made their way to France or to French settlements in Quebec and in Louisiana.

returned to the land they loved. The British, as the sole rulers of this part of North America, no longer felt threatened by the Acadians and permitted them to stay. The Acadians, however, found that immigrants from New England had settled their lands. So the Acadians moved farther away. Most of them made their homes along the eastern and northern shores of New Brunswick. Others settled along the St. John River. As the Acadians moved farther into present-day New Brunswick, they occupied Native lands. The Native peoples, in turn, moved farther inland, away from the fertile coastal lands and river valleys that had been their home.

To the south, the revolt of 13 colonies against the British launched the American Revolution (1775–1783). By the end of the Revolution, the colonies had won their independence and had formed the United States of America. Thousands of United Empire Loyalists—colonists who remained loyal to Britain—fled north to live in British territory. Nearly 8,000 Loyalists arrived at the mouth of the St. John River in 1783. Over the next several years, their numbers grew to almost 15,000.

Loyalists arrived in Parrtown in the spring of 1783. Over time immigrant settlements forced the Micmac and the Maliseet off their traditional lands and onto reserves (reservations). In addition, many Native people died from exposure to immigrant diseases, such as smallpox and typhus, to which they had no immunity.

Most Loyalists settled on the banks of the St. John on the north side of the Bay of Fundy. They called their community Parrtown, in honor of John Parr, the governor of Nova Scotia. (At that time, Nova Scotia still included present-day New Brunswick.) But the Loyalists worried about being persecuted for their loyalty to Britain by immigrants living on the south side of the bay. Many of these immigrants had come from New England and supported the

▶ New Brunswick was named in 1784 after the Duchy of Brunswick-Lüneburg, a region in Germany that Britain's King George III ruled at the time.

new U.S. government. So the Loyalists asked the British king to establish a new colony with a new governor. The king granted the request, and the colony of New Brunswick was born in June 1784. The next year, Parrtown became the city of Saint John—the first official city in what eventually became Canada.

Birth and Growth of the Port

Unlike the Acadians, who grew crops and raised animals to feed and clothe their own communities, the Loyalists were more interested in producing trade goods for the expanding international marketplace. Powerful countries such as Britain, France, and Spain had already claimed colonies in most parts of the world. They traded their colonies' natural resources (such as wood, gems, and spices) with other countries to earn money. They also continued to explore other lands looking for more and varied trade goods. Because wooden ships were the only means of travel in those days, wood became a very valuable natural resource.

The Loyalists realized they had the potential for great wealth in the form of lumber from New Brunswick's vast forests. Before long the Loyalists developed a very prosperous shipbuilding and lumber trade. Loggers cut giant trees in the forests of the interior and floated the logs down the St. John River to Saint John, which was a perfect natural port and the ideal place for building ships out of the logs. Soon lumber mills and shipyards were bustling with activity, and Saint John was off to a strong start as an important trading port.

In the early 1800s, New Brunswick began supplying Britain with lumber. The great white pines of New Brunswick produced straighter and longer pieces of lumber, which allowed shipbuilders to make larger ships than Britain had ever had. Ships built in Saint John helped Britain keep its place as the most powerful shipping and trading nation in the world.

By the mid-1800s, Saint John was building more ships than any other place in what is now Canada and ranked as the fourth largest shipbuilding port in the world. Many of the era's famous ships, such as the *Marco Polo* (considered the fastest ship in its day), were built in Saint John. The shipbuilding boom created a large number of jobs for shipbuilders, carpenters, sail-makers, and riggers (outfitters who supply equipment for a ship's sails and masts). All these jobs attracted a flood of immigrants from England, Ireland, and Scotland. Often the ships that transported lumber to Britain carried a return cargo of hundreds of immigrants.

> ▶ In 1843 most of the 156 ships registered in Liverpool, England, that weighed more than 500 tons had been built in Canada.

In the mid-1800s, shipyards in New Brunswick were producing more than 100 vessels each year. Much of the low-paid labor was provided by immigrants from Great Britain.

THE FATHER OF THE PORT

During the Port of Saint John's long history, the name of William Pugsley (1850–1925) stands out above all others. Born into a Loyalist family in Sussex, New Brunswick, Pugsley took a degree in law and spent 10 years working for the Supreme Court of Nova Scotia. In 1885 he returned to New Brunswick, where he served in the provincial government for many years before becoming New Brunswick's premier in 1907. After only a few months in that post, he resigned to accept the position of minister of public works in the Canadian federal government.

As minister of public works, Pugsley spearheaded construction of several new docks and piers at the Port of Saint John. He favored building the Navy Island bridge linking the east and west sides of Saint John. He also earmarked federal funds to pay for part of the cost of design work for the bridge. He pushed to develop the Courtenay Bay section of the harbor and to build a dry dock there. Pugsley was also instrumental in bringing additional railway service to the port. In honor of Pugsley's many contributions, authorities named Pugsley Terminal in the Main Harbor for the man who had accomplished so much for the Port of Saint John.

As the city of Saint John grew, so did the port. With an increasing population, the city needed more food, clothes, household furnishings, and other daily necessities, which Saint John's businesses began to import. In turn, the increasing demand for consumer goods created even more jobs and attracted even more people to the city. During the port's early years, Long Wharf was the center of all port activity. Just behind the wharf lay the city's business center, where lawyers and bankers had offices and where farmers and merchants sold their products.

In the 1850s, workers built a wharf at Reed's Point (the northern end of present-day Lower Cove Terminal) to serve the passenger steamships that were beginning to stop at Saint John. Soon passenger ships traveled regularly from Saint John to Digby and Halifax in Nova Scotia, as well as to Portland, Maine, and Boston, Massachusetts. A steam ferry also transported passengers across the harbor, linking the east and west sides of the city of Saint John.

◄ Railroads

When steel-hulled ships replaced wooden cargo vessels in the late 1800s, New Brunswick's shipbuilding boom came to a sudden end. Some Saint John shipbuilders began making steel-hulled ships, but city and port officials realized they had to find other ways to keep their economy alive.

Along with steel hulls came steel rails. Saint John, like many other cities of the time, began to dream of rail connections to other areas. Business leaders in the city knew that if they wanted to maintain a busy, prosperous port, they needed railways to transport goods overland to and from the docks. Meanwhile, the Province of Canada (present-day Ontario and Quebec) was already busy building railroads. One of these railroads, the Grand Trunk Railway, ran northeast from Toronto, Ontario, to Montreal, Quebec, with connections to Portland, Maine, on the Atlantic coast.

With rail service, the Port of Montreal on the banks of the St. Lawrence River was able to handle the region's export cargoes for much of the year. During the winter, however, Montreal was icebound, so Canadian cargo was shipped out of Portland instead. Saint John wanted to change this situation and become Canada's winter port. But first the city needed a rail connection to the Province of Canada. With financial help from the British government and private businesses in the United States, the European & North American Railway Company was formed to build a railway between Saint John and Shediac on New Brunswick's east coast. This was only a start. There was still a long way to go.

In the early 1860s, many leaders in both Britain and Canada favored the unification of the British colonies in what is now eastern Canada. At this time, both New Brunswick and Nova Scotia were trying to raise money to build railways. Officials in New Brunswick and in Nova Scotia thought that if the colonies agreed to unite, Britain might give them the money to complete railway construction. So in 1867, New Brunswick, Nova Scotia, Quebec, and Ontario entered into Confederation (the union of the colonies) as provinces of the new country called the Dominion of Canada.

A train crosses a rail bridge over the St. John River. Railways allowed farmers and manufacturers to move their products to the port quickly and efficiently.

At the same time, Saint John was working to improve port facilities. Workers renovated and strengthened wharves along the east side of the harbor, built new berths, widened dock aprons, and extended rail tracks right to the docks. In 1869 the European & North American Railway Company completed a railway that linked Saint John to Boston. Built on the west side of the city, the new railway encouraged port expansions on the west side of the harbor.

By 1876 workers had completed the Intercolonial Railway (ICR), which linked Canada's four provinces. But this railway didn't bring the prosperity that Saint John had expected. Instead it brought competition from the port of Halifax, Nova Scotia, which was also connected to Ontario and Quebec by the ICR. And rather than opening up new markets for New Brunswick's products, the railway flooded the province with cheaper goods from Ontario and Quebec.

Workers built a railway bridge in 1885 to link the east and west sides of the city. And by 1898, Saint John had earned official Canadian winter-port status and was operating year-round. Grain from the Canadian west, which was shipped through the Port of Montreal during the summer months, began to come to Saint John in the winter. The port had the added advantage of providing the shortest distance between Canadian farms and factories and European consumers.

The port built by lumber and shipbuilding industries was transforming into a grain-shipping port. To accommodate the grain shipments, workers built Saint John's first grain elevator on the west side of the harbor in 1893. A second elevator, located on the east side, followed shortly thereafter. At the same time, Saint John was slowly changing from a regional port, handling only local goods, to an international port for shipping products from all across Canada to the rest of the world.

The Port in the 1900s ▶ During World War I (1914–1918), Saint John played an important role in shipping vital

Saint John's waterfront bustled with activity during World War I.

Fire consumes a terminal in the 1930s. With many wooden structures, the port faced the constant threat of damaging fires.

munitions, food, and clothing to Canada's overseas troops. But Canadian soldiers didn't head to the war zones from Saint John because the shortest railway line from central Canada to Saint John passed through Maine. The United States, which did not enter the war until 1917, would not allow Canadian soldiers to cross its soil. Therefore, although war supplies were shipped through Saint John, Canadian troops departed from Halifax, Nova Scotia.

As Saint John gradually became involved in international shipping, organizations outside the city—such as the federal government, railway companies, and shipping lines—increasingly made decisions about running the port. In 1927 the Canadian government nationalized (took control and ownership of) the Port of Saint John, making it a federal port. The citizens of Saint John were proud that their port's importance to the nation had been recognized, although they regretted losing control of the port.

Nationalization came at a time when the port needed aid. In 1931 a devastating fire com-

In the 1930s, the Canadian government provided funding for a major construction project at Saint John to expand the port and to replace wooden facilities with structures that were less susceptible to fire.

pletely destroyed the entire west side of the harbor, which the city couldn't afford to rebuild. But the federal government, which had greater resources, immediately spent millions of dollars on reconstruction. The old wharves, which had been supported by wooden pilings and faced with wood, were replaced by state-of-the-art, fire-resistant concrete and steel structures. The improvements also left the port better equipped to handle increasing traffic.

The port's growth continued over the years. In 1934 workers finished a massive expansion project that added the 17-acre Navy Island terminal to the port. That same year, crews completed a new channel in the Main Harbor to replace the original Z-shaped channel, which had been quite difficult for ships to navigate. Between 1948 and 1952, workers rebuilt the Pugsley Terminal berths. Ten years later, crews completed extensive renovations to the Long Wharf Terminal as well.

Over the years, the port developed new types of import and export business. In the 1960s, for example, forest products became an increasingly valuable export product. These years also marked Saint John's entry into containerized shipping. In 1972 workers completed the Rodney Container Terminal on the west side of the Main Harbor. The new terminal gave the port increased capacity to handle containers, and by the mid-1970s, Saint John was servicing 13 container shipping lines.

In 1975 workers at the port constructed a forest-products storage shed specially designed for mechanized forklifts called liftjacks. With increased mechanization, fewer laborers were needed to handle forest products at the port. At about the same time, the trucking industry began to take away overland shipping business from railways as trucking companies offered lower fees and greater efficiency. The amount of cargo shipped by rail dropped off and fewer trains visited the port. A decade later, the port dedicated a separate terminal for handling potash—an increasingly important commodity for Saint John.

From its very beginning, the Port of Saint John has grown in size and in the amount of

> ➤ The Port of Saint John was the first port in the world to be listed on the Internet's World Wide Web. Visitors to the port's home page—www.sjport.com—can read about a range of topics, including shipping services, traffic volume, and tidal conditions at Saint John.

Officials hope to enhance the port's competitiveness and its diversity of services by seeking new business, maintaining a skilled workforce, and improving port technologies and vessel turnaround time.

business it does. The growth has occurred in response to the demands of the community—the city of Saint John, and to a lesser degree, the province of New Brunswick. The port is an important player in the economy of the city and of the province. Although trends in trade and shipping continue to change, community expectations of the port remain the same—to provide revenue and jobs. Therefore, the Port of Saint John continues to develop new and effective ways of ensuring a strong port economy for the future.

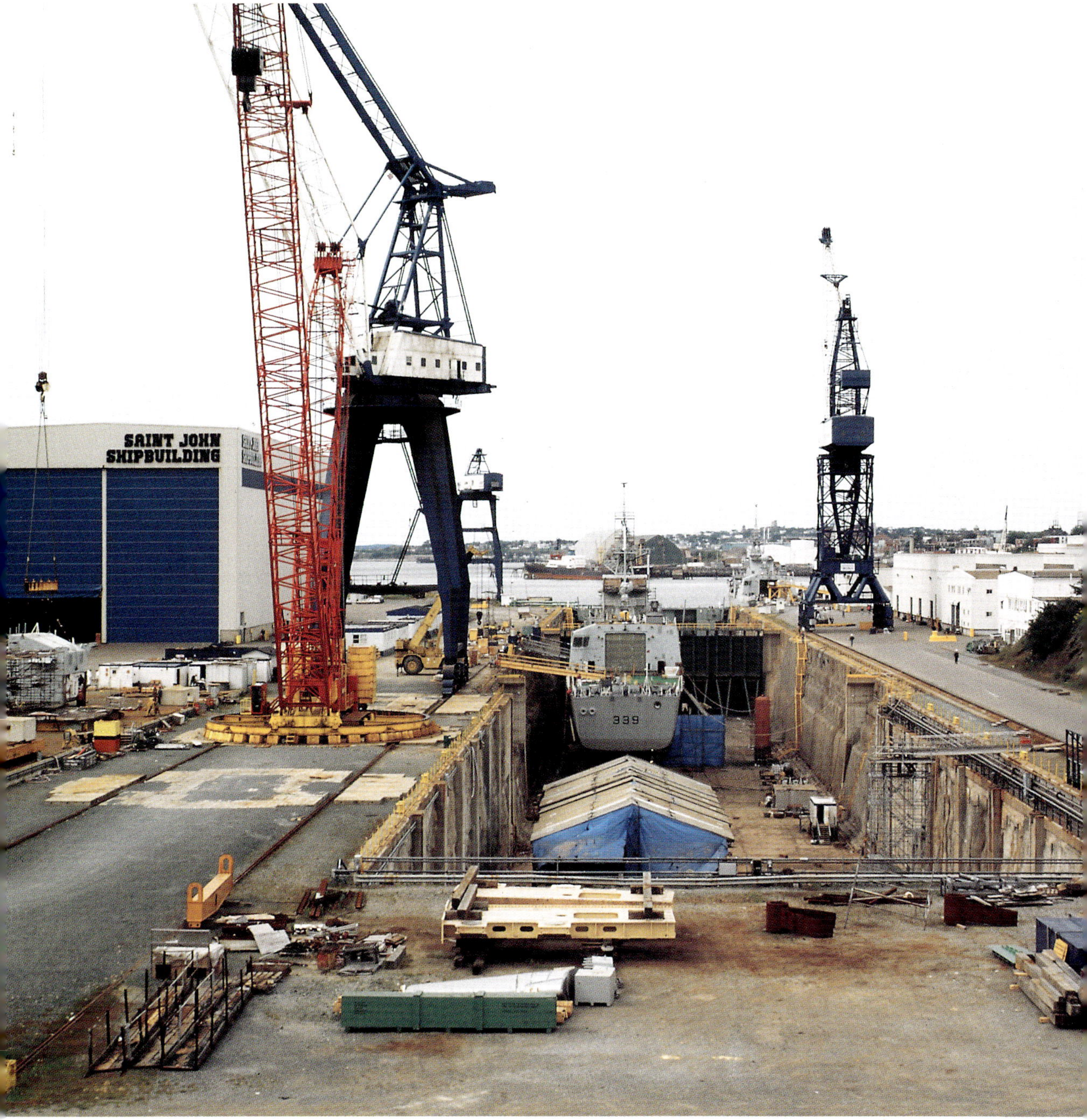
SAINT JOHN
SHIPBUILDING
339

CHAPTER THREE

THE PORT AT WORK

Ship repairs and assembly take place in sunken facilities called graving docks (facing page). *When the vessel is ready for launching, workers flood the dock until the water level in the dock is the same as that in the harbor. Workers then release the gate on the harbor side to allow the ship to exit.*

Trade has existed since very early in the history of human civilization. Early peoples lived in small groups and raised their own food and made their own clothes and tools. Over time communities grew larger and less self-sufficient. People realized that if they needed something they could not produce, they could trade with another community by bartering (exchanging) a product or service for the desired item. Bartering continued until coins were first minted in the 600s B.C. Currency (money) made trading much more convenient. Communities, and eventually whole nations, could trade with a wide variety of markets, using currency to purchase goods and services from a broader base of suppliers.

In general, nations produce raw materials and manufactured goods that are best suited to their climates, their economies, and the skills of their citizens. They trade these products for items they can't or don't have the technologies to produce. For instance, tea and coffee grow in tropical climates and cannot be cultivated in most of North America. Through trade, North Americans are able to enjoy these two popular beverages.

◀ **Trade Practices**

By producing and trading raw materials and manufactured goods that are valued by other nations, a country can earn money to buy products and services that its citizens need and want, thereby improving living conditions. Producing raw materials and manufacturing products on a large scale also create employment in the producing country. Large-scale manufacturing keeps production costs low, which leads to lower prices for consumers.

The more markets a producing nation can find for its goods, the more prosperous the nation will become. The most advantageous trade conditions occur when nations maintain a **balance of trade.** This balance is achieved when the value of a nation's exports (what it sells to other countries) is roughly equal to the value of its imports (what it buys from other countries). As competition increases, nations that export more than they import—thereby earning more than they spend—are generally considered to be economically powerful.

If a nation earns more from exports than it spends on imports, the country has a positive balance of trade. On the other hand, if the country spends more on imports than it earns on exports, it has a negative balance of trade. Overall, Canada maintains a healthy positive trade balance. To maintain a positive balance of trade, some nations, including Canada, impose tariffs or special duties (taxes) on imported goods. The import tariffs usually raise the price of foreign goods, protecting the importing country's own industries by ensuring that local consumers will purchase less costly, domestically produced goods. At the same time, governments may also impose export tariffs on materials that are in short supply within their own countries. Export tariffs, which make these materials more expensive, tend to prevent large-scale sales of raw materials. These tariffs help prevent depletion of scarce materials.

This system of imposing tariffs, called **protectionism,** can limit a country's economic growth and cause bad feelings among nations. To prevent these negative effects, some nations have formed free-trade communities in which tariffs are reduced or eliminated among member nations. In the mid-1990s, for instance, Britain and other countries in Europe formed the European Union (EU). At about the same time, the United States, Canada, and Mexico negotiated the North American Free Trade Agreement (NAFTA), which took effect in 1994. Under this treaty, goods and services will eventually flow among the three countries as though there were no borders between them.

NAFTA has yet to show a measurable impact on activities at the Port of Saint John. One reason is that the port historically has not done much all-water trading with the United States.

Most trade between Canada and the United States is handled by trucking companies, because overland transportation is faster than water travel. In addition, Mexico has never been one of Canada's major international trading partners.

Port authorities say that since the signing of NAFTA, overall Canadian trade with the United States and Mexico is increasing. The port hopes that this boost in traffic will lead to more opportunities for all-water shipping to both the United States and Mexico. The port also hopes to see the extension of the NAFTA agreement

President Bill Clinton (above) *signed the North American Free Trade Agreement in Washington, D.C., in 1993. The treaty went into effect the next year.* (Facing page) *Conveyor systems transfer potash from dockside warehouses to bulk carriers.*

to include Central and South America, which authorities feel would increase trade with the nations of this region.

EU regulations, on the other hand, have had a direct impact on Saint John and the businesses it serves. EU rules, for example, require lumber companies that sell their products to EU nations to dry the lumber in high-temperature ovens called kilns to kill off harmful insects. As a result, lumber companies in New Brunswick have had to increase their kiln-drying capabilities significantly. The EU has also set an annual quota (limit) on imported newsprint, and New Brunswick's share has gradually decreased as EU members meet more of the demand.

Political affairs across the globe also impact the Port of Saint John. After the Soviet Union collapsed in 1991, for example, Saint John's potash exports began to drop. The decline occurred because eastern European countries that were once allied with the former Soviet Union started to flood the port's traditional potash markets with the mineral. To earn valuable foreign currency and to capture all the potash markets, the eastern European nations sell their potash at very low prices—prices with which other countries can't compete. The practice of selling large volumes of a commodity at very low prices is called dumping.

Services and Cargoes ▶ The Port of Saint John is an important link in the trade routes of the eastern seaboard of North America. Situated on the Bay of Fundy, the port provides easy access to global markets, including the United States, which lies only an

51

hour away. At any given time, dockworkers handle cargoes from approximately 12 shipping lines that call regularly at the port. Every four weeks, for example, the port services carriers transporting containerized and **breakbulk cargo** (non-containerized, packaged commodities) to Australia and to various countries in Africa, the Middle East, and Asia. Dockworkers handle vessels carrying these same cargoes to Caribbean, Central American, and South American markets every week and ships stopping in Venezuela and other South American countries every three weeks. Business at the port also includes carriers transporting breakbulk cargoes to the United Kingdom, continental Europe, and to Egypt and other Mediterranean markets on a monthly basis. And every three weeks, port workers service cargoes bound for Japan, South Korea, and China—via the eastern seaboard of the United

A dockworker maneuvers a side-lifter into place to load breakbulk cargo onto a ship's elevator system.

Tall ships (above) *and cruise ships* (above right) *are among the many vessels that call on the Port of Saint John each year.*

States, through the Panama Canal in Central America, and then across the Pacific Ocean.

Besides managing cargo traffic, the Port of Saint John also hosts visits from about a dozen cruise ships every summer. Cruise-ship calls to the port are increasing every year. In the mid-1990s, the roster included visits by the *Queen Elizabeth 2*, the world's most famous cruise ship. The ocean liner can accommodate 1,700 passengers in addition to a crew of more than 1,000. Another high-profile event at Saint John is the visit of tall ships, a flotilla of sailing vessels patterned after ships built during the 1700s and 1800s. The ships—which come from Canada, the United States, Britain, and the Caribbean—visit several ports on the Atlantic seaboard each summer and rekindle memories of the age of sail.

FROM DUST TO DUST

Potash is the common name for a group of salts containing potassium, a key ingredient in chemical fertilizers. Manufacturers use potash mostly for making fertilizers, although a small percentage is used in soaps, detergents, glass, pharmaceutical drugs, and pulp and paper.

Half of the world's supply of potash is found in New Brunswick and Saskatchewan. New Brunswick's deposits lie as far as 3,200 feet below the ground in Sussex, about 45 miles east of Saint John. Workers at potash mines operate giant machines resembling drills to excavate potash ore at rates ranging from 330 to 550 tons per hour. Conveyor belts transfer the ore to mine shafts that raise buckets loaded with 22 to 28 tons of potash to the surface. Potash ore contains 40 percent potash, 55 percent salt, and 5 percent clay. Because the ore is not pure, it takes about three tons of ore to render one ton of potash.

Mills process the ore by crushing it and mixing it with a liquid brine. Large tanks then agitate the semiliquid mixture to remove clay and other materials. Next, the liquid is transferred to flotation tanks, where chemicals are added to coat the potash but not the salt. At this point, air is injected into the tanks to force the coated potash particles to rise to the top, where they are skimmed off.

The potash particles are then dried, crushed, and sorted by size. Trains carry the potash from the mines to the Port of Saint John. At the Barrack Point terminal, doors in the bottom of the railcars open to dump the potash into large pits. Conveyor belts then carry the potash into two huge warehouses that can each store a little more than 66,000 tons. When bulk carriers arrive at the terminal for loading, conveyor belts transfer the potash to vessels heading to markets all over the world. Factories buy the potash and mix it with nitrogen and phosphate to make a variety of fertilizers. Farmers and gardeners spread fertilizers in their fields, and the potash goes right back into the earth!

Traffic and revenues at the Port of Saint John continue to grow each year. In 1996 the port experienced a banner year, with an increase in tonnage of all commodities. Total port volume rose from 19.8 million tons in 1995 to 23.5 million tons in 1996. Petroleum, which accounted for 19.1 million tons in 1996, is the main cargo at the Port of Saint John in terms of volume. Most of the petroleum is crude (unrefined) oil and comes from Norway, Saudi Arabia, and Nova Scotia. A major refinery in Saint John processes the crude oil into fuel oil, gasoline, and other petroleum products. Trucks and ships then take the fuel to gas stations and other distributors in the Maritime Provinces of Canada and in New England.

Potash from New Brunswick is Saint John's second ranking product, with 1.8 million tons passing through the port in 1996. Potash is exported to a wide range of global markets, including Australia and various countries in Europe, South and Central America, and Africa.

Petroleum and potash (above) *are Saint John's top cargoes in terms of volume. Tugboats guide an oil tanker into position* (below).

55

The Navy Island Forest Products Terminal is one of the largest forest products terminals on the East Coast of North America. The terminal's inventory, shipping, and billing systems are all computerized.

Pulp and other forest products remain a major export, ranking third highest in volume and providing the largest number of related jobs. Forest products come not only from New Brunswick but also from Ontario, Quebec, Nova Scotia, Manitoba, and Maine. In 1996 about 1.1 million tons of forest products, in the form of wood pulp and paper, were shipped from the port to buyers in Germany, Brazil, China, France, India, Saudi Arabia, and many other nations around the globe.

Current trends in shipping encourage vessels to make fewer stops en route to market. As a result, cargoes from smaller centers are shipped overland to ports such as Saint John—known as load centers—that are equipped to handle large volumes of cargo. By stopping only at the load centers, ships and shipping companies save time and money.

Apart from the standard cargoes that Saint John manages on a regular basis, the port is also called upon to handle unusual cargoes from time to time. For example, the port ships beef and dairy cattle from New Brunswick to the

➤ The Navy Island Forest Products Terminal can handle up to seven ships at a time.

> The Irving Oil refinery is the largest refinery in eastern North America.

Saint John handles a variety of breakbulk cargoes, including non-containerized goods as well as a wide range of heavy-lift items, such as flight simulators, tractors, military tanks, and hydrocrackers (below) *and other oil-refining units.*

United Kingdom and Puerto Rico. Several shipments are often required to get all the cattle to their destinations. Saint John also handles the annual shipment from England of military equipment to supply the training needs of an entire regiment at a British military training base in Alberta. Once a year, the used equipment is shipped back to England to be repaired, while a shipment of new equipment arrives to replace it. A typical load could include tanks, jeeps, armored vehicles, and 150 or more containers of assorted military supplies.

The Port of Saint John is outfitted with specialized lifting systems to handle heavy, oversized cargoes. In 1995, for example, a giant piece of equipment called a hydrocracker arrived at the port for the Irving Oil refinery. The 608-ton hydrocracker splits petroleum molecules to produce a highly refined, low-sulfur diesel fuel for large transport trucks. Workers maneuvered special cranes to unload this extremely heavy unit.

The Port of Saint John is busier as an export port than it is as an import port. Although petroleum—the single most important commodity for Saint John in terms of volume—is both an import and an export product, the next three highest ranking commodities (potash, forestry products, and salt) are all export items. Most of the remaining traffic at the port (containers and breakbulk cargo) is also made up of export items.

Port authorities are acutely aware of this imbalance in the port's trade patterns and are actively seeking to balance the situation by adding to their import volumes. For instance, officials are looking for a product that can be imported in the bulk carriers that come empty to pick up outgoing potash shipments. The port is confident that as activity continues to grow, import cargoes will increase as well.

▶ Each year the Port of Saint John handles about 322,500 tons of New Brunswick salt, which ranks as the port's fourth largest commodity in terms of volume.

▶ Conveyor equipment at Saint John can load salt onto ships at the rate of 1,320 tons per hour.

◀ Port Management

The Port of Saint John is managed by a federal government corporation called the Saint John Port Corporation, which is governed by a board of directors. The board is made up of local citizens who make the major decisions concerning the port. The port's president, along with staff members, carries out these decisions. Because port property belongs to the federal government, the port corporation has some obligations to the Canadian government. But in general, the port corporation runs its own operations.

In 1987 the port corporation replaced the Harbor Commission, which had run the port's operations for 60 years. In the mid-1990s, the Canadian government wanted to eliminate the

Pleasure craft share the docks with tugboats and military vessels.

expense of maintaining its ports. The government's plan is to give the ports back to the communities in which they are located. In the future, therefore, the people of Saint John will once again manage the port, much as they did when it first came into existence more than 200 years ago.

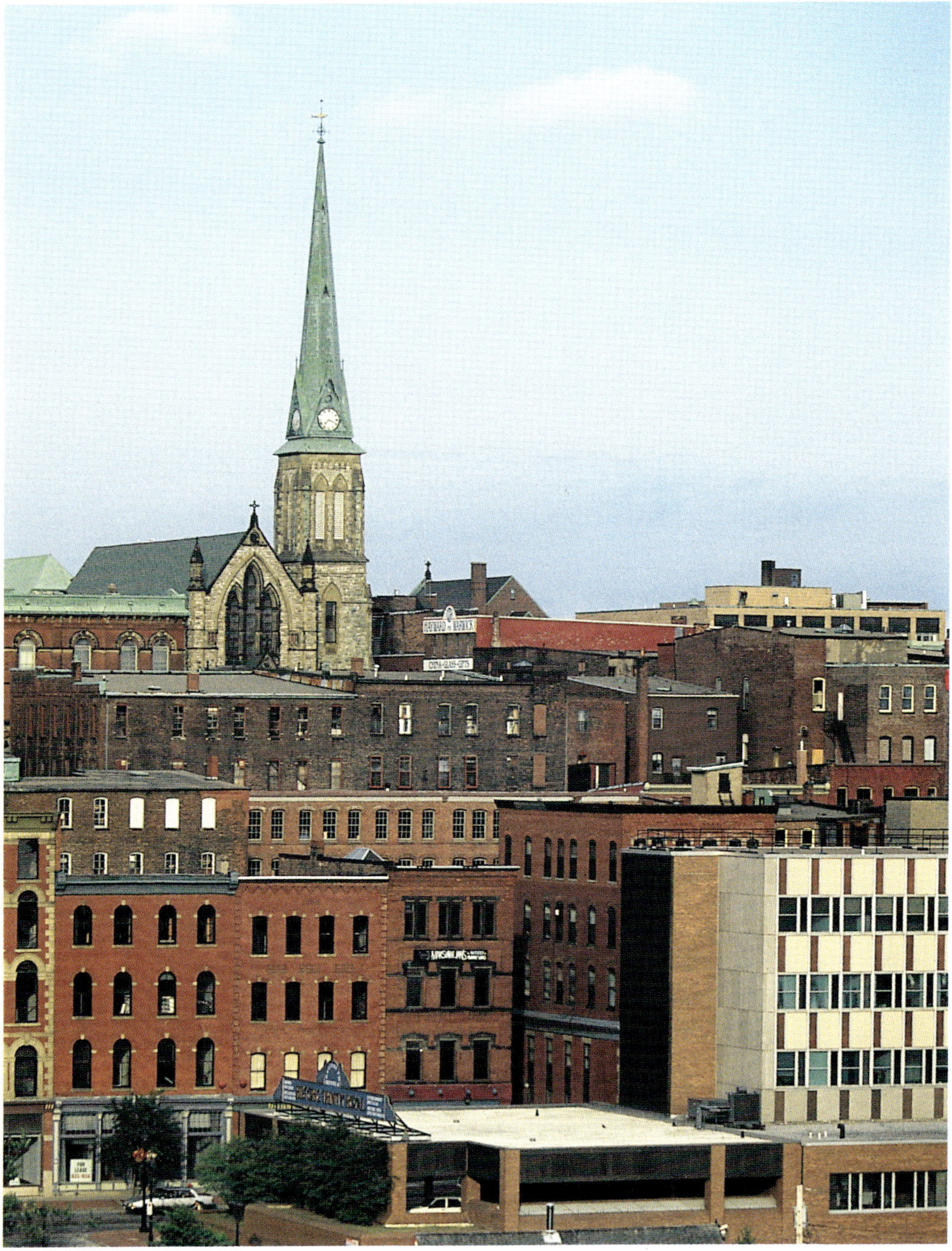

CHAPTER FOUR

LOYALIST CITY

Saint John (facing page) *is New Brunswick's most populous city.*

Life in the city of Saint John has always been closely intertwined with the port. From its earliest days, the port has had a great deal of influence on the prosperity of the city. In return, city administrators have taken a keen interest in the port's progress and well-being.

Saint John is a thriving business center with a population of 130,300 people. From the city's Loyalist beginnings, the community has blossomed into a vibrant business and cultural center that is fast becoming Atlantic Canada's most popular city in which to live and work. In 1996 Canada's *Report on Business Magazine* chose Saint John for the second time as the nation's Premier City for Business. During that same year, the Canadian Federation of Independent

Business identified Saint John as The Best Business City in Atlantic Canada.

A superior transportation system—which includes the port, two railway networks, an international airport, and an efficient trucking industry—plays a major role in the business world's attraction to Saint John. Businesspeople also appreciate Saint John's skilled labor force, the city's proximity to markets for buying raw materials and for selling products, and the availability of critical services such as electrical power and efficient communications networks.

Added to these services is the city's quality of life, which makes Saint John an appealing place to live. An excellent education system, good health services, beautiful land and seascapes, attractive homes, a variety of cultural and recreational activities, and a high level of personal safety are among the city's most important features. Saint Johners are considered to be some of the friendliest, most cooperative, and positive people in Atlantic Canada. They believe in

A young New Brunswicker gives a friendly wave.

The Irish Festival—Canada's oldest and largest Irish cultural event—takes place each year in Miramichi, New Brunswick, which lies to the northeast of Saint John.

working together to make their city prosper. These traits go back a long way, and many historians have credited them for the prosperity of the community.

A Diverse City ▶ Although Loyalists played an important role in the founding of Saint John, they were not alone in developing it into a modern urban area. The Irish and Scottish immigrants who followed the Loyalists in the 1700s and other groups have contributed a great deal to the character of New Brunswick's largest city.

In the 1990s, the city's ethnic mix consists of the descendants of these British cultures and of the early Acadians. More recent additions include peoples from Chinese, East Indian, Ethiopian, Somalian, and various mainland European cultures. Residents with British ancestors make up almost 46 percent of the city's population, while people with French backgrounds account for about 7 percent of Saint John's citizens. The city's black population, many of whose ancestors fled slavery in the United States, constitute about 3 percent of the community's residents. People of German, Canadian, Italian, Chinese, or Aboriginal (Native) backgrounds make up about 2.5 percent of the population. The remaining Saint Johners are of multiple origins.

The first section of Saint John to be settled by Europeans in the late 1700s was the east bank of the St. John River. This area remains the city center. Over time the city expanded farther to the east and west, as well as to the north, forming many suburban neighborhoods. In the late 1990s, more than 200 years after it was founded, Saint John covers an area of 125 square miles and ranks as Canada's second largest municipality in area.

Although some of the oldest sections of Saint John's original residential areas have fallen into disrepair, many of the historic homes have been refurbished to their former splendor. And while new subdivisions have grown up more recently on the outskirts of the city, especially around lakes and waterways, Saint John still supports a vital residential community in the city center.

New Brunswick is Canada's only officially bilingual province, offering all provincial government services in both French and in English.

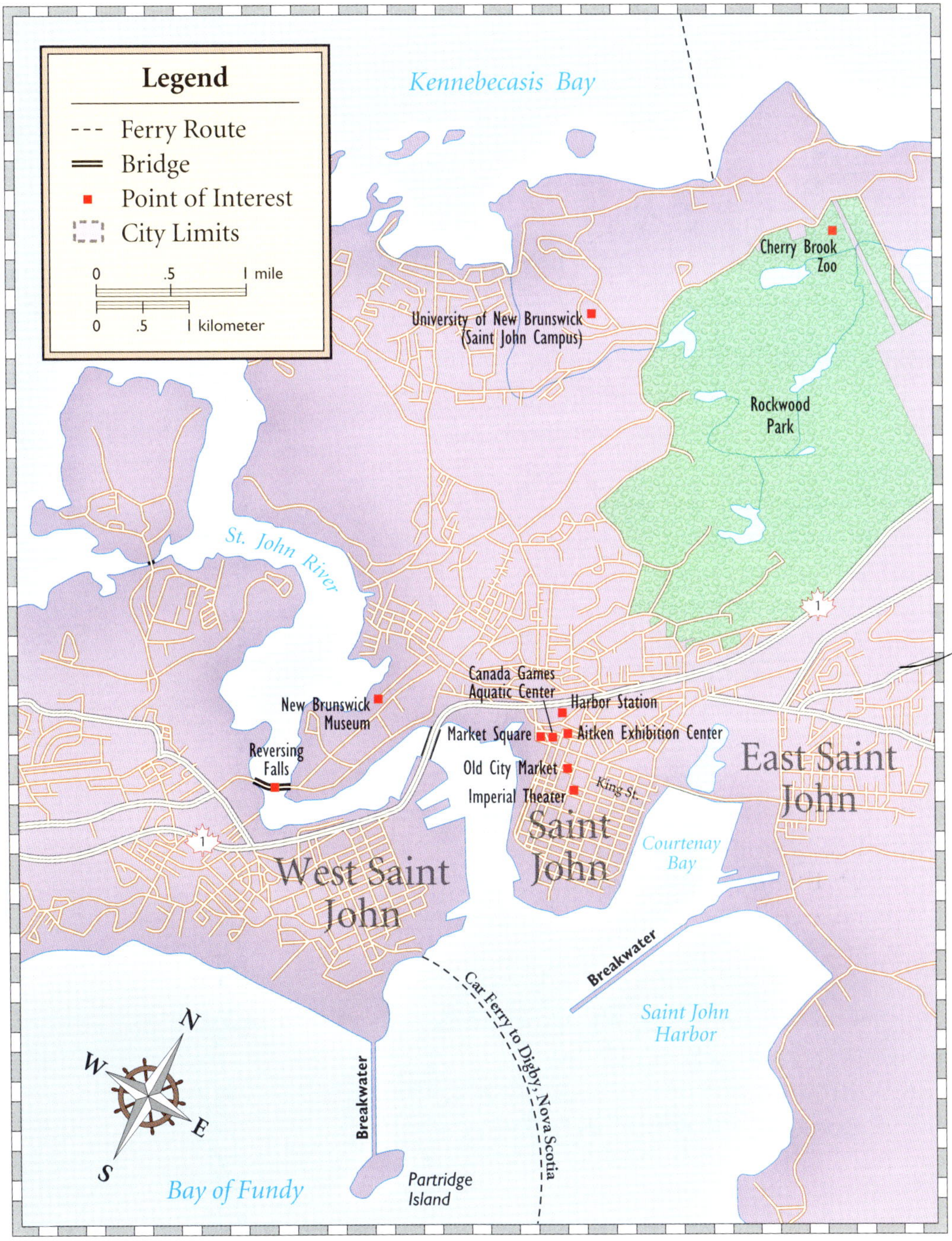
Legend
Ferry Route
Bridge
Point of Interest
City Limits
0 .5 1 mile
0 .5 1 kilometer
Kennebecasis Bay
Cherry Brook Zoo
University of New Brunswick (Saint John Campus)
Rockwood Park
St. John River
Canada Games Aquatic Center
Harbor Station
New Brunswick Museum
Market Square
Aitken Exhibition Center
Reversing Falls
Old City Market
Imperial Theater
King St.
East Saint John
Saint John
Courtenay Bay
West Saint John
Breakwater
Car Ferry to Digby, Nova Scotia
Saint John Harbor
N
W
E
S
Breakwater
Bay of Fundy
Partridge Island

Saint Johners enjoy sailing on the Kennebecasis River, one of the many bodies of water that surround the city.

Most of Saint John's heavy industry is located in East Saint John, a section of the municipality lying close to the port. The city's major industries include petroleum and sugar refining, shipbuilding, the manufacture of pulp and paper, and power generation. As in most cities, the chief government offices are located in the downtown area.

In a pattern similar to the trend in other North American urban regions, the growth of large suburban shopping malls has caused many businesses from Saint John's traditional central shopping district to move to the outskirts of the city. Smaller upscale specialty stores have replaced the large consumer stores in the downtown area.

One of Saint John's most attractive features is Rockwood Park, a large green space in the northeastern part of the city. Stretching across 2,200 acres of wooded land, Rockwood is Canada's largest municipal park and a place where Saint Johners can experience nature almost in their own urban backyards. Camping,

Outdoor Activities and Entertainment

> The Bay of Fundy ecosystem is home to a variety of fascinating wildlife, including starfish, sea urchins, harbor seals, porpoises, whales, and nearly 240 species of migratory birds.

Home to diverse species of marine life, Irving Nature Park provides visitors with an excellent introduction to the unique ecosystem of the Bay of Fundy.

hiking, and bird-watching are popular outdoor activities at Rockwood. The park also offers a wide range of recreational opportunities including swimming, boating, golfing, and mountain biking. During the winter, the park is a good place for skating and cross-country skiing.

Located at the edge of Rockwood Park is Cherry Brook Zoo—the only exotic animal zoo in Atlantic Canada. Cherry Brook houses many endangered species from around the world, including brown lemurs, golden lion tamarins, and wildebeests.

The Irving family donated the land for Irving Nature Park, a 556-acre wildlife park located along the western shorefront of the city. The nature park is a great favorite of Saint Johners for bird-watching, hiking, and cross-country skiing in the winter. Pugsley Park is a good place to view port activities at the Main Harbor. Another natural feature of great interest to residents and visitors alike is the Reversing Falls at the mouth of the St. John River. At high tide, twice each day, the powerful action of the Fundy tides causes water to flow into the river's mouth with such force that it actually travels up the rapids.

Saint John's waterways offer a variety of attractions. A windsurfer on the Kennebecasis River pulls his sail into place (below). *Visitors head to the Reversing Falls on the St. John River* (left) *at high tide to watch the waters of the Bay of Fundy travel up the river.*

Surrounded by the Bay of Fundy, several lakes, and the St. John and Kennebecasis Rivers, city residents have no shortage of both saltwater and freshwater beaches during the summer months. Sailing, boating, and windsurfing are popular recreational water activities among Saint Johners.

In addition to a wide range of outdoor recreational opportunities, Saint John also boasts several indoor sport and recreational facilities, including the Canada Games Aquatic Center and the Canada Games Stadium. Located in the heart of the city, the Aquatic Center offers swimming pools, water slides, whirlpools, saunas, and state-of-the-art exercise equipment.

A colorful collection of old-time goods grace the display windows of Barbour's General Store in downtown Saint John.

The stadium, which is located on the University of New Brunswick campus, is one of the finest track-and-field facilities in Canada. It features an eight-lane all-weather running track, a natural grass interior, and seating for 8,500 spectators.

Saint John often credits its reputation as one of eastern Canada's foremost cultural centers to its Loyalist ancestors. With a love of music and theater, the Loyalists went to great lengths to develop these arts in their new home. Centuries later, in keeping with the wider ethnic makeup of the city, Saint John's music, theater, and dance performances tend to have a more multicultural flavor. The Imperial Theater—restored to its 1913 splendor and providing high-quality sound and lighting equipment—is the home of Theater New Brunswick, Symphony New Brunswick, and the Saint John String Quartet.

Saint John's exhibition centers offer a variety of activities. The Harbor Station facility, home of the American Hockey League's Saint John Flames, is one of Atlantic Canada's most popular performance spaces for concerts, exhibitions, trade shows, and conventions. The six galleries of the Aitken Bicentennial Exhibition Center feature a range of art and science exhibits, many of them part of national or international tours.

Saint John offers ample insight into its past. Visitors to Barbour's General Store, for example, can wander through this old-fashioned country store and enjoy guided historic walking tours through the neighborhood. Saint John also has a number of cemeteries dating back to the late

1700s. Historic homes, churches, and museums dot the city. These museums include the New Brunswick Museum—Canada's oldest—as well as a Jewish historical museum and a firefighters' museum.

The University of New Brunswick campus in Saint John opened in 1964, although Loyalists founded the main campus in Fredericton (the province's capital) much earlier—in 1785. The newer campus continues to be an important educational institution in Saint John, with 1,900 full-time students and 1,400 part-time students. Another educational institution in Saint John, New Brunswick Community College, offers vocational training and programs in various technologies for 3,500 students each year.

Saint John has long been considered the industrial hub not only of New Brunswick but of Atlantic Canada as a whole. The city contributes more than one-third of New Brunswick's gross provincial product (the total value

◀ **Saint John's Labor Force**

The University of New Brunswick has campuses in Saint John (below) *and at Fredericton.*

Fishing boats moor in a small harbor near Saint John.

> ➤ Fishers in the Bay of Fundy haul in lobsters, snow crabs, and sardines.
>
> ➤ Saint John is New Brunswick's largest community and Canada's oldest city.

of goods and services produced annually by provincial workers). Some of Atlantic Canada's largest companies—including Irving-owned companies, The New Brunswick Telephone Company, New Brunswick Power, and Moosehead Breweries—have thrived in the city for decades and have spearheaded Saint John's reputation as a hub of industrial activity.

About 16 percent of Saint John's workers have jobs in manufacturing industries, which include oil and sugar refineries, shipyards, and pulp and paper mills. Close to 6.5 percent of the city's labor force are employed building roads, homes, office towers, and other construction projects. New Brunswick's mineral resources earn a lot of money, but overall, primary industries (mining, farming, forestry, and fishing) furnish jobs for fewer than 2 percent of Saint John's labor force. Most working

71

people in the city—75.9 percent—have jobs in the service sector, which provides consumers with services rather than products. Service workers include teachers, doctors, waiters, tour guides, truck drivers, ship captains, and various government employees.

Saint Johners who work aboard the ferries that cross the Bay of Fundy are part of the city's large service sector.

In a city that grew up around its harbor, the port continues to be vital to the economy of Saint John. Although the Saint John Port Corporation employs only 25 people, port operations provide jobs for thousands of people who work for various companies that do business there. The port also generates millions of dollars in annual revenue for the city. For example, the port buys materials, products, and services from local firms; hires individuals and companies to render services; and pays grants for provincial and municipal taxes. In turn, the

Truckers provide a vital service to the Port of Saint John, which relies on overland transportation to haul goods to and from the docks.

▶ Two railway companies link the Port of Saint John to other parts of Canada and to the United States. The Canadian National Railway serves the terminals on the eastern side of the port, while the New Brunswick Southern Railroad provides trackage on the western side of the port.

employees who provide services to the port spend their earnings on products and services that create more employment. These individuals also pay taxes to all three levels of government.

The Port of Saint John has the most impact on two main areas of the city's economy—the overland transportation sector (trucking and railways) and the general service sector. Because many of the raw materials and products that pass through the port need to be transported overland to and from the docks, many jobs are created in both the trucking and the railway industries. The general service sector includes all the businesses that provide services to the port. Customhouse brokers, for example, arrange for imported cargo to be delivered to buyers. Chandlers supply ships with food, clothing, and any

A tugboat pushes a barge out of Saint John Harbor.

other equipment that crews may need. Bunkering services supply ships with fuel. Also included in this sector are towing companies that provide tugboat services, harbor pilots to guide ships into their berths, and marine surveyors and cargo inspectors to inspect vessels and their cargoes.

The longshoremen who load and unload ships are also members of the port's service sector, as are the warehouse operators who store cargoes. Ship repair services are considered part of the service industry, too.

The cargoes that account for the largest volume of port activity don't necessarily create the most jobs at the port, however. For example, petroleum products account for almost 83 percent of total port tonnage but only generate 33 percent of port jobs. On the other hand, general cargo (containers, wood products, pulp, paper, and steel) makes up only 7 percent of port tonnage but provides 44 percent of port-related employment. This disparity occurs because petroleum products require very little handling

Cranes load paper products aboard a ship. Port officials feel confident they are well positioned to meet the challenges of doing business in the age of technology.

by workers en route to market. In contrast, general cargo requires many more workers to get from one place to another.

As the Port of Saint John moves into the twenty-first century, port officials and city leaders realize that many changes lie ahead—changes in port management, in technology, and in world trading practices. Nevertheless, port and city officials are optimistic that they will handle these challenges successfully, and that the port will move smoothly into another century as an important link in international trade.

GLOSSARY

apron: The space between a berth and storage sheds.

balance of trade: The difference over time between the value of a country's imports and its exports.

breakbulk cargo: A term used to refer to non-containerized general cargo. This cargo category includes items packaged in separate units, such as boxes, cases, and pallets, as well as heavy machinery that is too big to be transported in a container.

breakwater: A seawall that protects a harbor from strong waves and currents.

bulk cargo: Raw products, such as grains and minerals, that are not packaged in separate units. Dry bulk cargo is typically piled loosely in a ship's cargo holds, while liquid bulk cargo is piped into a vessel's storage tanks.

dike: A containment wall or dam built to prevent waterways or undesirable materials from overflowing.

dry dock: A dock where a vessel is kept out of the water so that repairs can be made to the parts that lie below the water line.

freshet: An overflow or a rise of the water level in a river or stream caused by heavy rains or melting snow.

Saint John's Old City Market is a favorite shopping spot. Built in 1876, the market runs the length of a city block.

gantry crane: A crane mounted on a platform supported by a framed structure. The crane runs on parallel tracks so it can span or rise above a ship to load and unload heavy cargo.

general cargo: Cargo that is not shipped in bulk. This cargo category includes containerized and breakbulk cargo.

peninsula: A stretch of land that is surrounded by water on three sides.

protectionism: A trade philosophy of protecting a nation's domestic companies by controlling trade with other countries through trade barriers such as quotas and import taxes.

PRONUNCIATION GUIDE

Acadia	uh-KAY-dee-uh
Algonquian	al-GAHN-kwee-uhn
Cartier, Jacques	kahr-TYAY, ZHAHK
Champlain, Samuel de	shaw^n-PLA^n, sah-mew-EHL duh
Courtenay	KOHRT-nee
de Monts, Pierre du Gua	duh MOH^n, PYEHR doo GAH
Kennebecasis	keh-nuh-buh-KAY-sihs
Maliseet	MA-luh-seet
Micmac	MIHK-mak

INDEX

Acadia and Acadians, 30–33, 35, 64
American Revolution, 33
arts and recreation, 9, 66–69
Atlantic Ocean, 7, 29

balance of trade, 48
Barrack Point Potash Terminal, 21, 54
British North America, 32–35

Canada, Dominion of, 39
Canaport Marine Terminal, 23
Cape Breton Island, 32
cargo, 9, 14–21, 52–53, 56–57, 74
Cartier, Jacques, 29
Champlain, Samuel de, 30
channels, 23–24
Cherry Brook Zoo, 67
climate, 8
commercial fishing, 9
containerization, 18–19, 44
Courtenay Bay, 10, 21–23, 37

de Monts, Pierre du Gua, 30
dredging, 23–25

Eastern Woodlands Algonquian people, 27–29
environmental concerns, 25
ethnic diversity, 63–64
European Union (EU), 49, 51

exports, 15–16, 19, 41, 44, 48, 55–58

ferry service, 9, 21, 38
fishing, 9, 29–30
Flowerpot Rocks, 26–27
forestry products, 15–17, 44, 56
Fort La Tour, 32
France, 29, 32
Fundy, Bay of, 7–9, 13, 21, 27, 30, 34, 67, 68

gantry cranes, 15, 18–19
grain, 41

Henry IV, 30
higher education, 70
history, 27–45; British control, 32–35; European settlers, 30–35; French explorers, 29–32; growth of port, 35–41; Native peoples, 27–29, 30, 31, 34; 1900s, 41–45

immigration, 34, 36
imports, 20, 23, 48, 58
industry, 66, 70–72
international trade, 41, 48–53
Internet listing, 44
Irish Festival, 63
Irving companies, 22–23, 57
Irving Nature Park, 67

Kennebecasis River, 66, 68

labor force, 70–75
Lantic Sugar, 14

La Tour, Charles de, 32
Long Wharf Terminal, 16–17, 44
Louisbourg Fortress, 32
Lower Cove Terminal, 14
Loyalists. See United Empire Loyalists

Main Harbor, 10, 14, 16, 23, 44
Maliseet, 27–29, 31, 34
maps, 2, 11, 65
Maritime Provinces, 7
Micmac, 27–30, 34

nationalization of the port, 42–43
Navy Island, 29, 37
Navy Island Forest Products Terminal, 16, 18, 29, 44, 56
New Brunswick, 7–8, 15–16, 21, 25, 27, 30, 32–36, 38–40, 51, 54, 70–71
No. 11/12 Terminal, 20
North American Free Trade Agreement (NAFTA), 49–50

Outer Harbor, 10, 13, 22–23

Parrtown, 34
petroleum, 14, 22, 55, 58, 74
Port of St. John: description of, 7–11; economy, 70–75; facilities, 10, 13–23; future outlook, 45, 75; history of, 27–45; map of, 11; trade, 47–59

Port Royal, 30
potash, 21–22, 51, 54–55, 58
protectionism, 49
Pugsley Park, 67
Pugsley Terminal, 15, 37, 44
Pugsley, William, 37

railroads, *See* trains
reefer containers, 19–20
Reversing Falls, 68
Rockwood Park, 66
Rodney Container Terminal, 18–20, 44
ro–ro vessels, 9, 17–18

St. Croix River, 30
Saint John, 61–75; business climate, 61–62; city map of, 65; economy, 61–62, 72–75; employment, 70–75; ethnic diversity, 63–64; population, 61

Saint John Harbor, 10
Saint John Port Corporation, 13, 24–25, 58, 72
St. John River, 7, 12, 24, 32–33, 35, 66, 68
St. John River Valley, 27
Saint John String Quartet, 69
St. Lawrence, Gulf of, 29
St. Lawrence River, 29, 39
Seven Years' War, 32
shipbuilding, 22–23, 35–36, 38
Symphony New Brunswick, 69

tariffs, 49
Theater New Brunswick, 69
tidal waters, 12–13, 68
tourism, 14–15, 53
trade, 35–38, 44–45, 47–59

trains, 38–41, 73
transportation, 38–41, 62, 73
Treaty of Utrecht, 32

United Empire Loyalists, 33–35, 63

Woolastook River (St. John River), 30
World War I, 41–42

METRIC CONVERSION CHART

WHEN YOU KNOW	MULTIPLY BY	TO FIND
inches	2.54	centimeters
feet	0.3048	meters
miles	1.609	kilometers
square feet	0.0929	square meters
square miles	2.59	square kilometers
acres	0.4047	hectares
pounds	0.454	kilograms
tons	0.9072	metric tons
bushels	0.0352	cubic meters
gallons	3.7854	liters

ABOUT THE AUTHOR

Kumari Campbell owns a marketing and public relations business and is a co-owner (along with her husband) of a tea room called The Carousel, in Clear Springs, Prince Edward Island, where she is the manager and chef for four months each summer. Campbell has worked as a technical writer for more than 20 years and has written three books—*As the Feller Says, Prince Edward Island,* and *New Brunswick.* The latter two titles are part of Lerner's Hello Canada series for young readers. Campbell lives with her husband and the youngest of their three children near Souris, Prince Edward Island.

ACKNOWLEDGMENTS

I would like to acknowledge the very valuable assistance I received from the following people during the process of researching and writing *Destination Saint John.* My warmest appreciation goes to both Ken Krauter and Adam McBride, who welcomed me with open arms when I first embarked on this project. General manager and assistant general manager, respectively, of the Saint John Port Corporation when I visited Saint John, they generously spent countless hours with me, giving me valuable insights, patiently answering my questions, taking me on an extensive tour of the port, and plying me with reams of literature.

Allen Fraser and Ed Vye, also from the port corporation, were most helpful and generous with their time. I also offer my thanks to Tom McGloan, who willingly shared his experiences both as a practitioner of admiralty law in the city and as one-time chair of the Saint John Port Commission. Terrence Totten, city manager, sent me valuable information on the city, as did Lisa Young of Enterprise Saint John. Ms. Young undoubtedly was an invaluable asset to her city. Darlene Lamey of Proud of Race Unity Dignity through Education provided me with insightful information on New Brunswick's black population. Mary Keith of J. D. Irving furnished me with information about her company, as did Roger Albert for the New Brunswick division of the Potash Corporation of Saskatchewan, Inc. Elizabeth McGahan's book, *The Port of Saint John: From Confederation to Nationalization 1867–1927,* provided important insights into the history of the port. And finally, a word of thanks for someone from my own province—Brian Scales of Island Fertilizer, Ltd., who most generously provided me with information on the manufacture of fertilizer.

Last, but not least, my heartfelt gratitude for someone without whom this book would not be what it is—my editor, Domenica Di Piazza. As often is the case, these unsung yeomen work behind the scenes with little public recognition, caring only that the final product is the best.